MONSTERS AND OTHER LOVERS

LISA GLATT

MONSTERS AND OTHER LOVERS

Pearl
Editions

LONG BEACH, CALIFORNIA

The author gratefully acknowledges the following publications, in which some of the poems in this book previously appeared:

The Wormwood Review, Chiron Review, Tsunami, ONTHEBUS, 420, Blank Gun Silencer, xib, Pearl, Genre, The New Los Angeles Poets, A New Geography of Poets, Truth and Lies That Press For Life: Sixty Los Angeles Poets, Stand Up Poetry, and *Poetas de Los Angeles.*

With gratitude to The MacDowell Colony, Djerassi, Headlands Center for the Arts, The Ludwig Vogelstein Foundation, and Yaddo.

A special thank you to Gerald Locklin, Thomas Lux, and Wendy Griffin, and to my editors Marilyn Johnson and Joan Jobe Smith.

Cover design by Marilyn Johnson

Cover illustration by Francis Poole

First Edition

ISBN 1-888219-00-9

Pearl Editions
3030 E. Second Street
Long Beach, California 90803
U.S.A.

For my mother . . .

"Where is the ebullient infinite woman who—immersed as she was in her naiveté, kept in the dark about herself, led into self-disdain by the great arm of parental-conjugal phallocentrism—hasn't been ashamed of her strength? Who, surprised and horrified by the fantastic tumult of her drives, hasn't accused herself of being a monster?"

—*Hélène Cixous*

CONTENTS

1. *Where I First Ate Love*

2. *69 Rose Street*

3. Woman Without Skin

4. Monsters and Other Lovers

I. WHERE I FIRST ATE LOVE

What the Fast Girl Says

I have always been afraid
of my breasts. I was twelve
with my hand in my red nightgown
feeling them, convinced even then
that what they were
was cancer, not some fine
puberty. I masturbated
with a playing card, the ace
of spades between my legs, the ace
becoming blurry, all I could not see
or experience or understand. I understood
this: what pleased the boys
would one day kill me. It was simple,
my aunts went one
after the other
and had their parts
scooped out, and each
returned to her man
with a twisted look
on her face, each said, Forgive
what I look like
now, each hid her skin
in her own red gown. What happens
when little girls are caught destroying
the family games, like cards? We played
Scrabble, Operation, and Life, and I was always
in a corner, beating my ears, losing,
losing my bright mothers one at a time,
each with a different wig
while my own breasts grew,
and when the boys reached out,
I undid my bra. *This*
is what the fast girl says
when in the back
of some blue Chevy,
she says, Touch them,
touch them while they're here.

In This Foul Alley

It is noon and cloudy, like night
already, and we are standing
in the alley behind our bar,
we are standing in the alley
with our dead, your two brothers,
newly men and Gone, each of my bald aunts,
their tossed hills and twisted lips.

You tell me about your boys
again, their last ride, how
every year in a rented red car
you drive toward Palm Springs,
sit with a bottle of Jim Beam
at that damn dinosaur
where it happened.

We have been fucking for six months
and do not love each other.
We can't somehow.

My mother sat on the couch
Sunday night, sewing my dark skirt,
saying, When the pain comes
I want you to kill me. She said this
simply, easily, like a demand
for more cold tea. When it comes,
she said, taking the needle
from her mouth, I want
to go. And I want

to go, too, standing with you now
in this foul alley, I want *to go.*
You press me against the red brick
and, of course, my panties dampen,
of course, I can never be
your brothers alive, and no matter
what you do to my breasts in the night

4

you cannot make them kind. They are
your favorite part of me, and yes,
I admit, breasts in my family
are beautiful and deceiving, high
and firm, temporary as fruit.

I cannot fuck the grief
out of you; you cannot
soothe it out of me.
And this will end soon.

But now, before the rain comes,
unsnap my black bra, lean down,
curl your spine, kiss. Kiss.

I Will See Their Teeth

Fifteen years ago my mother was
a nudist, tan and slim, eating
Chinese food with the liberals
in Topanga after the park closed.

On Thursdays and Fridays she walked
our hallways, swinging her full breasts,
trying to teach me pride, this life,
acceptance. I was twelve, my body
confusing me—nothing grew on time
or looked the way I wanted. I refused
to see her, the finished product,
was embarrassed that her body
wasn't perfect, hated the strange veins
on her legs, those dark nipples, all
that was around my corner. *Parents shame you
when you're young,* she said. *If I'd been religious
you would have hated God.* Today my mother is

a patient, Cedars-Sinai, room 333.
Across the room a TV gives us the election
results. She is still groggy from drugs,
yet concerned. *Bill is the future,* she murmurs.
Did the sexy one win? They have carved

her left breast from her body,
taken it, tossed it, left it
in some bin with other diseased pieces
or taken it out back for the dogs.

I first ate love there, I want to say,
but don't, because this story is not
yet about me. Later
I will undress for him,

offering my own breasts, those
two liars. And while he bends down
to touch them with his mouth, I
will hear the neighbor's dogs
barking, growling; I will see
their teeth.

What We Did
After My Mother's Mastectomy

We didn't sleep.
Three nights we sat up
in her bed, watching bad talk shows,
the same news again and again. We stayed
there, our shoulders and twin hips
touching, the sheets twisted, four bare feet . . .

We could have been anyone: man and woman,
girlhood friends, lovers. We could have been
at any point in time, any age, her
in her thirties
with an Afro, a husband,
and hot pants, me
looking like a boy
at twelve, resenting
her body, her soft legs
and arms, hating the ease
with which she pinched off
her bra, and the breasts
set free then
for all the world.

But we were fifty-five
and thirty, mother
and daughter, two women
in bed, awake, three a.m.,
our eyes open, four a.m., our lips
parted, mouths dry, five a.m., staring
at the ceiling, and she said, *Your brother*
was a better baby, funny, and then
we stared in silence, at the ceiling,
at the yellow ceiling, paid attention,
watched the cracks, listened,
and waited.

My Mother as Humpty Dumpty

So much is about milk
and thirst and falls and guilt
and eggs. Take her, standing in the mirror
with her rubber breast
in her hand, with her lipstick
on. *I want my body*
back, she says. He stood
with two balls, a head of curls, and all
that education, carving, then
patted my head, saying, *Things look bad,*
Honey. I was not his

Honey. I was not my father's
Honey. I was no one's Honey,
standing in that white hallway in Beverly Hills,
watching Audrey Hepburn's irises pile up.

Tonight, I sit on the wall
with all my fragility
watching her watch
herself. We laugh
that there's no nipple,
no fat baby to feed.

There are things she does not know: how I've stood
in storefront windows, watching women
5'9" and plastic, wanting any body
but my own, how I've held scissors
to my wrists, how I've crouched in an alley
with a giggling man in my mouth, throwing
my body away. Now,
my mother and I
do everything

to put her body
back together. We glue
the rubber breast
to her skin. We hold
the rubber breast
in place

until
it sticks.

School Teacher's Breast Cancer

I was terrified
that she was hairless,
afraid of her skull
and vagina, her eyes minus
brows and lashes, her alien manner.

At night
while she slept
I crept in.

The red wig hung on the globe
beside her bed—
the whole earth
where her face
would be
in the morning.

Bugs

At first, he is delicate, offering her this option. Coaxing, kind, like a man in the beginning. He stands at her bedside, flips through her chart, and nearly smiles.

When she squirms, his jaw sets, his manner changes. Now, like a boy in a back seat talking about his balls, he says, *Blue, it's turning blue.*

She moans and mumbles something.

We could always remove it, he says. *Or . . .*

She is afraid of bugs, not the way we're all afraid, but deep inside, and I remember her screaming when a huge noisy fly landed on her arm, when red ants found our kitchen, and once, on a family vacation to Hawaii, a flying cockroach skimmed her cheek, and I remember what she wore—a red halter dress, I remember her naked legs, the humidity, the fat moon, my step-father's laugh, but mostly, I remember the *exact shriek,* its pierce, pitch—I was twelve, I think, and she was my mother, young, slim and tan, screaming for her life.

Leech

One would fit in the palm of your hand
if you opened it. He would sit there

across your lifeline, an interruption.
Squirming with gustatory delight, he'd smell

your skin before he was introduced.
It's not about beauty, she says, *but symmetry,*

balance. When she stands in her red stockings
her two feet aren't planted firmly. She falls off

her bike, cracking her chin, and refuses
new men and escalators. Now, I notice

the veins in her neck, her blue gown,
her one true breast. The hair, like they

promised, has come back in curls. The rest
they will not say, offering statistics, a shrug,

oily desserts. She is fluid as milk and I
am always her small girl, sitting by the window,

angry, my throat scratched raw from wanting
her. *You were a bad baby,* she says, *always*

dissatisfied. And he, with his rough wool sweater,
stethoscope, and job to do, ignores us,

opening his can of worms.

On the Night They Apply
Leeches to My Mother's Makeshift Breast
I Take You Into My Mouth

Willing as I once was, eager, noble,
and it seems your blood is calling
specifically my name, and to that
I bend and open, my long hair
to one side, my clever jaw.

It is here, like this,
you trust
I have come back to you.

It is here, like this,
you trust
I will not eat you whole.

Across town in a metal bed
my mother is trusting too, sitting up
with worms on her new breast, reading
Cancervive. Every day is stunning,
she said earlier. *They're greedy
but generous as well.* And you believed her,
and believe her now, your back arched
and grateful. Still, you fight
the urge to fit your hand
in my curls and guide me,
wanting even tonight to make
your own decisions.

My last man wouldn't touch me,
wanted me clothed
in my floral robe, my mouth
open. I told you
on our first dinner out

how he ruined the act itself, how
he taught me about thieves, sour milk,
and starvation, how giving up everything
made me want sharp teeth, and he

is here now, a vapor, all his lessons,
his fair hair and grin, his coy
thank you's. *Me,* you say quietly,
it's about me. Yes, I tell you,
raising my eyes, my mouth still full
of you, *I know.*

The Feeding

Where once she offered
me milk,
she offers him
blood. Sitting up
in hospital sheets,
she feeds him
from her bluish breast.

Later, when fat,
he'll be flipped
into a pile
with his satiated cousins
to die. Imagine
his last moments.
How wonderful! Purple mouth
open. Thick. Rich. Drunk.
Body plump with mother.

Maturation

In the beginning the breast is stingy and uncertain, congested, and he, having not eaten in six months, is impatient, greedy. While she sleeps, he escapes from under the gauze like a one night stand, slithers up her body and finds her ripe neck. He sucks where we'd suck if invited, traveling from breast to neck like a lover. Below her ear he scores dinner.

Eventually, feeling his pressure, she wakes. And screams. Nurse Kate, comfortable with needles, squirming humans, vomit, and excretions, screams as well. Finally, another nurse joins them. *What's the fuss?* she says, peeling the sneaky worm from my mother's neck. *God damn,* she growls, *grow up.*

Greed

They are slick and wet, full of hunger, like Him, who left with his
paunch, a sloppy beard, my mother's diamond studs in one hand, a
two-breasted gal in the other, who left

with the smallest piece of steak between his molars, his hot tongue
grabbing, twirling at the pesky sirloin, who left, looking back only for
a moment, saying, *I need a toothpick,*

then adding, like an afterthought: I wasn't happy *before this.* But
they, *they* are happy, admitting what they want from her. Dark
mouths open, confessing their gluttony,

they plump with every red drop. She cannot refuse such honesty,
desire. Imagine someone, anyone, that loyal.

Pride

Tonight, I climb on top of him
specifically to show them off.

I tell him how shy I was before,
how I hid them in my bra
when I was with the others.

After my mother's breast
was carved away, my own breasts
became beautiful, perfect,
like a man you meet
from another country
who plans to return there
without you.

My hands clasped behind
my head now, my neck arched
and yellow in this light.

Killer

He eats meat.
Red meat.
Extra red.
Nearly raw, so that the blood
drips down his chin, falling
on the collar of his bright white shirt.

I want to know how he gets his shirts
that clean. Leaning over, I say,
What do you use?

He only wants to talk about
my breasts. *They're high
for being big,* he says.

They're killer, in fact. He swallows
the red piece in his mouth, stares
right at them.

The pasta is hard, smelling
on the plate in front of me.
His eyes are dark blue.
And this is a time
for meat. And more meat.

Across town my mother wears
bright colored wigs. My aunts
are lopsided, and I am one
of two selfishly fearful nieces.

Yes, I say, moving
a piece of hair
behind my ear, *they're
killer, yes.*

Magic

Each hand, each coarse palm, holds one, and he
stares, the faint light from the nightstand shining just

enough. Satisfied with what he sees, he presses them together
like an accordian, skin and nipples, nerves and blood,

presses them together until I become a pin-up girl, a gaudy dancer
he does not know. My face, neck, and shoulders could simply

disappear, and he is solid, moving fast between them.
They are dry, I keeping thinking, *he is not inside anyone.*

I ask him later over beer and sourdough, over spinach
and rich cheese, what it's like for him. And he says, *Like I'm alone*

with your tits, and they're no longer attached to you—like they're
completely mine. Sounds bloody, I say. He rips a piece

of bread from the loaf. *No,* he tells me, raising the crust
to his lips, *no knives, it's magic.*

Cancer

A woman in a red nightgown. A fraction
of her breast exposed. She feels
cool air on that fraction
of her breast. The skin there is white,
whiter than the rest of her.

Her bra is lace, black, and hangs
over a chair; she sees
only half of it.

Outside there is one slice
of moon, two moody dogs.

The man who does not love her enough
sleeps beside her. His pampered camera
on the table. In the morning
he will take pictures
of spiders, boulders, her pretty feet.

She touches his arm, wanting things
from him: stamina, lies, a glass of milk.

She listens to him breathe.

Her mother is Gone now.
And each of her aunts.
Only the girls.

She listens to him breathe
and wishes herself angular.
A triangle or cube.

She cups her breasts.

Every night now
she is waiting.

2. 69 ROSE STREET

Monsters

My first grade teacher, Miss Wilder,
was old and thick, with brown spots
on her arms and hands. She had a hump
on her back the size of a throw pillow.

She barely lifted her head, taught us
to spell and add, which state we lived in,
with her chin on her chest, moving
only her eyes.

Taking roll, she pronounced my name wrong.
Glutt, she said, Lisa Glutt?

Daily, I curled in my chair,
giving her the smallest "here" possible.

The cutest boys called her The Hunchback.

The day I was hit by a car
those boys finally came
to see me. They stood
where I'd been hit, looking
at my skin and blood, at what
I'd left behind.

I don't know what they said,
those cute boys, if they
grimaced and transformed, if they
knelt, their palms
and bones in the street,
and heard us monsters calling.

Nudity

When the doctor removed a cast
I was clothed; when I bathed
my leg was hidden.

He would take one cast off,
look at my twisted foot,
and quickly slap plaster around it.

When I was twelve
my mother became a nudist
and, together with my step-father,
joined a camp.

On Thursdays and Fridays
my friends weren't allowed
over. Thursdays and Fridays
were Naked Days
and my parents walked
the halls of our home.

I remember
my mother's high breasts,
my step-father's
uncut penis.

I remember
waiting
for pubic hair.

I remember
waiting
to see my leg.

Weird Leg

It is very skinny and white, whiter
than the rest of me. The toes are
permanently curled. When doctors gather
around the leg, they hold
their yellow beards and say, *It looks
remarkably like polio.* They smack clipboards
against their thighs and say, *We should have thought
about atrophy.*

I am surprised each time
the doctor leans down
and saws a cast,
removing it. I am surprised
each time by two things: (1) that yet
another cast is being prepared—I see
the rolls of plaster
smoking in the sink. And (2) the way
the leg smells. The way
the leg smells.

69 Rose Street

We scratched the walls
in that house
like the mice
who left dark stones.

We were naked, wanting out,
wanting cheese, wanting protection
from our own tiny claws.

Our humiliations were unique
as they happened
without our clothing.

His tongue
in my mouth
was never enough.

Mice are filthy, he'd say,
setting the trap
in the kitchen corner.

Mornings I'd watch him
fry eggs with determination,
his hairy fingers and ass,
my own broken yolks
a certain sign
of my impatience
and coming excitability.

Wait, he said. *Can't you wait?*

When I flipped them
I inadvertently stabbed them,
their yellow softness spilling over,
quickly burning, turning hard
and tasteless.

We were nothing like the neighbors
or so I thought
though on Sundays
we stood in similar driveways
with our car doors ajar,
chatting. Beach, lunch, church, park,
nudist camp. Four smiles for the ones
next door, the ones he hated most,
their crime a simple proximity,
what they might have heard
or even seen, how the tallest fence
could not protect
his uncut penis, her doomed breast,
or my own halted development.

I watched Claire in a perfumed skirt
follow her Christian parents
into their sedan. I wanted her
Sunday, her God and
grinning mother. I wanted
her noisy little shoes,
but most of all
I wanted her mouth,
those plump reddish lips,
the way they pulled perfectly away
from her teeth when she smiled,
and the tiny bit of rosy gum
revealed then
like the freshest, slightest
of mistakes.

Privacy

—for Carolyn Jacobs

I wanted to scratch my leg. I was sitting on my bed with a coat hanger in my hand. I was trying to get the coat hanger inside my cast, pushing the side of the cast into my calf, making room for the hanger, when my step-father opened my door.

"What are you doing?" he said.

"My leg itches. I'm trying to scratch it."

"It's dangerous. The doctor told you not to stick anything inside the cast."

"The doctor isn't here," I said, pulling the hanger out of the cast, setting it on my sheets. "I'm being careful."

"You could hurt yourself."

"Yes," I said.

"Try not to think about it. Think about something else," he said. "What if you think about something else?"

I was becoming more and more uncomfortable. As long as he stood in my doorway, watching me, I couldn't scratch myself.

"Can I be alone?" I said. "Please, I want to be alone."

"Your mother wouldn't like it," he said, closing the door.

Once alone, I pushed the side of the cast into my calf, moved the hanger in and out, scratched and scratched until the itch went away.

Real Girl

I was thirteen and didn't have pubic hair. Claire, my Christian friend, was twelve and had plenty. I thought God had given her that, that perfect hairy spot. By ignoring my pagan mound, I thought God was rejecting me. I stopped peeing with Claire, stopped inviting her in, used the bathroom alone—where, as you know, little girls and many women prefer company, where little girls and many women can talk with their legs and minds wide open. All year I peed alone and talked angrily in pink rooms to a God I barely believed in.

The real problem came when my brother Andy suggested a neighborhood game of Truth or Dare. And I, ever curious, agreed. We invited Claire and her brother. We were all under sixteen and had little Truth to tell, so we quickly advanced to the Dares.

I Dared first and Raymond eagerly showed himself. He was proud with a freckled belly. He was long and bold and hairy. Heredity, I thought, until Andy dropped his jeans to the carpet and smiled. Claire was next. She stood in front of us and slowly peeled her light blue pants from her curved hips. The pants sat in a circle at Claire's feet for what seemed to me longer than the required ten seconds. I felt my stomach turn; a tiny sound of envy came from my throat.

Now it was my turn. What was I to do? I imagined myself— the small mole and pale hairs. Raymond opened his mouth. I said I had to pee.

To this day I'm not quite sure what prompted me up the stairs and into my mother's bathroom and make-up kit, what made me reach in and grab that pink tube like a model might, and sit on the toilet, and with that black wand paint myself, mascara myself, darken what was blond and young and invisible. I curled my spine and blew myself dry.

Upstairs, I made the three of them keep their distance, then pulled my cotton skirt up, my cotton panties down. I counted to

ten. Claire, Raymond, and Andy stared right at it. I looked at
Raymond's grin.

That night, I went to Andy's room and knocked.

"Come in," he said.

I sat on the edge of his bed. He pulled the pink blanket to his
neck, rubbed his chin with the silk corner.

"Did it work?" I asked him.

"Man," he said, "you looked like a real girl."

Meat

My mother is sitting at the table with her chin in her hand, with her fingers on her cheek. My step-father is telling her to go on, to tell me about the dream she had about my leg.

Go on, he says again, tell her.

I'm tired, my mother says.

Your mother dreamed about hamburger meat, he begins. And in her dream you were seventeen, not twelve, and you loved a man. The man was older, say twenty, and you wanted to have sex with the man, but were too upset about your skinny leg. So your mother got hamburger meat from the freezer, and carried the meat to your room, and placed the meat on your skinny calf while you slept, and held it there, like that, until the meat stuck. Your mother did this so you could have sex with the man and not be . . . Do you understand? he says.

I am standing in the hall.

My mother's face is gone behind her hands.

Sweet

On Sundays my step-father made his baked spaghetti. It was a bland, dry dish that he was very proud of. Had he seen my mother at the counter with her plate of food, with her sugar packet ripped open, with the sugar on top of his dish like a white hill, with her fork mixing the sugar into his carefully spiced tomato sauce, he would have been incensed.

I discovered her there at the counter, like a guilty girl, and until that moment, no one had known her secret, or if anyone knew, he or she didn't mention it. Her behavior with sugar was her private habit, like the blue and yellow pills she took to keep her awake and thin, and she wanted no one, not even me, to find her out. I did the right thing when I returned to the dining room table with the can of cheese and looked at my brother and step-father blankly, not uttering a word about what I had seen.

Within time, my reward became apparent; my mother grew comfortable around me, and sugared her food, her beef, her baked chicken, her salad dressings, easily and often, secure that I would not judge her, secure in knowing that I lived there too, that I understood the sweetness she needed was necessary.

The World in My Mother's Hair

My mother hates her life
and dyes her hair—nearly daily, at least
two or three times a week. I call
and she says, "Call me back. I'm right
in the middle of a new color—Burnt Ruby."

My mother hates her life
and believes that Burnt Ruby
will bring her man back
to the bedroom, on his knees,
with the word yes
on his hot, red tongue.

My mother imagines his return
will change things—the way
I see her: At noon with a cup of tea
sitting on the plaid couch
with one hand on the cat and the other
shaking as she reaches for the cup—
in the evening with her head
bent, over the kitchen sink,
with the douche-like bottle
poised, with her scalp
burning, with her scalp
pleading, with her scalp
and all of its demands.

My mother thinks
his return
will cure her hypertension,
will cheer the cat,
will make the neighbors
take notice of her shiny hair.

One of Us

We opened up with each other in the afternoons as easily as we did nightly with the boys who did not know us. On Mondays we sat in Angela's den, six of us, eating Frosted Flakes directly out of the box. We passed her father's magazines around, *Playboy* and *Penthouse,* running our fingers over the glossy photographs, the woman's round breasts and perfect triangle, and we knew that the boys themselves were down the block or across town, staring at the very same woman in the very same magazine, and even then I wondered aloud, *Who is looking at them?* We sent Angela into Safeway to buy *Playgirl,* so we could see them. And as we stared at the pretty boys with their generous portions, we pretended we were happy; we pretended we did not miss *her.* But here's the thing, we *wanted* to look at the woman, she was beautiful and stinging in a way the naked men were not, she held our secrets in her terrible, lovely body, and we believed, by the very fact she'd posed and opened, she was one of us.

Whores

—for Jessica, Jenna, and Lolo

I met girls like me at school. Our fathers crept into our rooms at night or they didn't. We lived with two parents, one parent, or unwilling grandparents. We had a dog we loved or a fish we flushed when no one was looking. Our mothers had breast cancer or were healthy, running off to tennis. They stood at stoves, stirring creamy soups or ordered pizza five nights a week. Our fathers were corporate lawyers or waiters. We lived in big homes overlooking the ocean or we lived in cramped apartments with one too many relatives. We found each other smoking in bathroom stalls or at church, rolling our eyes or on our sincere knees. We found each other in the school cafeteria, refusing chocolate or devouring piece after piece of fudgy cake. We were pretty or we weren't. We had clear faces or we had acne. We picked our pimples until they bled or we used expensive creams, praying that we didn't scar. We had codes, a gutsy walk, an intrepid laugh, a relationship to our own flesh which drew us together, and we'd stand in knowing circles, with high IQs and important hair, waking them up.

I Was Once a Bell

I am sitting by the window.
I am biting my nails.
I want to shave my head.
I want to masturbate.
These are just symptoms, he said.

Outside, the sun is fat, orange
and poison. I remember sitting
in the sun, a girl, praising it.
I called it God.

A tiny boy on a bike rides by.
He thinks the sun is his friend
and waves to it
when no one's looking. He pedals
without a shirt.
His chest is pink.
Later, he will blister.

I remember when I liked boys.
Now the men come dancing
and leave before noon
without their legs. I was once
a bell, ringing in my purple shoes.
I was once a bell. I was once
a bell, I think.

The boy rides by again, this time
without hands. I remember risk, crossing
hot streets in only my stockings. Now,
no boots are thick enough
and I am biting my nails.
I am pulling skin from my fingers.
He hated my unoriginal habits, said I held back,
didn't give enough, said I couldn't act

for shit, and
blaming me
for even the rain, stood
at the car, holding
a broken umbrella. I wanted

to fix it, to ring
for him. I did. I tried. He tried
everything with those fancy hands
and questions. *Who wouldn't leave,* he said,
when every interaction becomes
a chore? I was once

a bell. And I rang.
I remember ringing
in my purple shoes.

Favors

I have stood with bottled water
in my purse, with my legs
open or in a knot
over some boy who calls me
Friend. What's more simple
than a grown woman in a crib
with urine on her twisted foot?

He asked me things—that I pee
on his chest, and that I could not do, not
in a year when I knew him better, not ever, not
after four glasses of water or wine.

No, I said.

What will happen to us, he asked,
if we don't do each other favors?

I think of him now, all that begging,
and am relieved—but the way
he opened my doors, the yellow one
made of wood, the red one
of hot skin, I know
I'll never regret
a boy like that.

He said, Your leg looks like a question mark,
then he bent down
and touched it
with his mouth.

What a Kid Could Live Through

Three years after I showed him
my leg, David said, My shoulder hurts. My shoulder
hurts. And they said, Pulled muscle—perhaps
it was the guitar, those punk songs,
or the way you lifted that fork
to your mouth. So hungry.

When they removed the bone, sold
his drum set, left him a mushy limb
and a scowl, his mother used my name,
my leg, my odd walk, as an example
of what a kid could live through.

I was in college
then, in Hawaii. I sent him
a postcard of a woman
in a grass skirt
with bare breasts.

What do you look like
now? he said on the phone.

You promised, I said.

A month before he died
his mother stopped using my name.
She stopped talking about me
at all.

Giving Charles Bukowski My Leg

Like a dead father
he comes to me
in the night, sits
at the foot of my bed,
wanting things.

Like a dead father
he's ready to know me
now, only after the worms
have covered his rich face.

*It's so much easier
to want you from here,* he says.

I would bend over
if he even hinted
but it's not my ass
he wants; it's my leg.

And because I am nothing
without it, because
it is scarred and small,
because I need it
to walk, *because of this,*
I unscrew it at the knee,
offering him
my calf, ankle, and foot.
All my ugly things.

Ugly, he agrees.

And he is beautiful
then, opening his hand,
holding it, he is beautiful,
touching my few dark hairs,

lifting my weird leg
to the light, beautiful,
I tell you,
more beautiful
than any one
of my smooth skinned boys.

3. WOMAN WITHOUT SKIN

Woman Without Skin

> *"Sometimes, the skin comes off in sex. The people
> merge skinless. The body loses its boundaries."*
> —Andrea Dworkin

For a while, sometime between
dropping the denim to the carpet
and the orgasm itself
we were both skinless.

I lifted my face
from between his legs
and saw the pinkish glow
that comes from blood and veins and muscle and juice.

Then, at some point,
when I wasn't looking,
he put on
his skin.

I sit on the edge
of this motel bed
with my skinless legs
parted. Our come drips
out of me; our salts burn
this body, this weird, red form.

I twist my juicy neck
to him.

I see
his back—two red bumps, five dark hairs,
and a mole.

Maps

I hate maps.
I don't read them.
Looking that hard hurts me.
If he slips one on my lap
I'll set it on the dashboard
without apology. *If this is love
we'll travel well together,* he said.

I know maps are necessary
and am grateful when others
read them. I prefer driving.
Just name the freeways and streets,
tell me which way to turn, and when.

He wants me to like maps. Last week
standing in my living room
in white boxers and thick socks,
he opened one up, his finger
traveling the paper, pausing
at each state we planned
to visit. *Here and here
and here.*

Once I stop moving
nothing in me
is as it was.

*Are you afraid
to arrive alone?* he said.

He thinks I hate maps
for the same reason
I can't come
no matter what he does
in the night
with his pretty tools.

All last month he begged me
with his mouth and fingers
and stamina. I thought of pretending
for his benefit, but decided
we'd only be further lost.

Knowing how I'm going
where I'm going
is too final.

Tonight, my pink bags are packed.
The moon is one weak slice. I sit
at the window, pull the curtain
each time I think I hear him
braking in my driveway. What is it

about motel rooms that causes
such collision? Every need is met there
and still my throat is parched.
No ice bucket the right color.
Each morning, as a numbered door closes
behind us, half of me stays behind,
sits on an unmade bed without my skin.

All the rules were made
to kill
a girl like me.

I want to come.
I have watched his face near mine
curling and twitching
with such finality
and I have thought: I want
to go there.

Why so many men, he said,
if you never come? The slut in me
knows how to knit. She fries eggs
in her white panties. She understands
the bad landscapes on motel walls
and despises subtraction.

In the car, after many patient hours,
his mask grows a face. He turns
and glares and whispers, *What is it
about maps?* And I answer, *Tiny lines
and arrows, all that blue, the miles
which are not miles, this road, this bridge,
this highway, that unsteady yellow light,
the getting where I'm going,
what I will become
once I'm there.*

One Night With a Stranger at 30

He moves his hips
and the lies we've told, the ring
he's hidden in his shirt pocket, that I've
never, these lies
and more
solidify, then go liquid,
and later, when sober
we will hold coffee cups
that do not match. We are not
anxious kids
who will curtsy politely
in the morning, our thirty years
here, the simple repetition
of this, what it doesn't
mean, our bold nudity,
a limited conversation, talk
about the map
above my bed, going
nowhere, his bright blue condom—
The fat girl moon
is meant to be romantic, he says.
If he were someone else, if I were,
I would tell him
how hot
these sheets are
with grief, how the dust
has crept back, how I wanted
to be someone else
by now, full of love, how I thought
I would be, how sometimes
making soup
or standing in the shower
I almost
believe I am.

I Am Weird to the New Boys

Six months
he sat in a wheelchair
and now near some valley
he coughs up dirt. Cancer made his kneecap
lunch and I'm eating Hormel chili at half past eight.
When you write for a living
and no one buys your words
canned foods grow appetizing
as the young poet
with black hair, holding
a notebook and waiting for me. He stands
on the corner of Argonne and Ocean in 1979
waiting so that together we can screw
the light bulb in—so that maybe
my cranky mother will smile at us. Smile David Mom meet smile. Oh,
the doctor is concerned about syntax—he wants
to understand something. If he's looking for dinner
on this white sheet then perhaps
he should take up trout fishing instead.

David wrote poems
called them punk songs
then he got sick, bald, and skinny. Who goes
on his eighteenth birthday with a yellow grandpa face? Who sells
his skis, gives away his brawling boots and two legs
and dies anyway? All summer I buried
my face in his perfect crotch. We waited
for the flies to stop buzzing. One circled
above my head, explaining things to me
while I discovered oral sex
and fell in love without my genitals. Yes,
I gave him that before he left in his sour boat.
If you believe he sits up in his coffin
choking on the dirt, remembering my name

you're more a poet or fool than I am. Quick,
grab your jacket
and chemicals. Leave the toothpaste home.
I won't ask you
to be David. I swear
your thighs are your own.
Bring them with you.
Show them to me.

Want

I eat
a diet pill
because David
left my sheets.

I eat
a diet pill
because a biology teacher
who I slept with
told me fat's yellow
and stinks.

I eat
a diet pill
trying to block out
the hunger I
do not want. Fifteen years ago
my brother Andy was a fat
little boy. My mom
gave him a diet pill. The next day,
though he'd lost a pound, he
wouldn't take another. She asked
him why. Andy said, "I want
to be hungry."

The Things We Do Alone

I write about masturbation
and death. The man who loves God
hates me, calls me Satan. The man who loves God
is never alone. God sleeps
in his pocket. God tells him things,
censors his love life and
literature. I tell the man who loves God
about David's yellow tumors. They said
he was too sick, that a picnic
in my blue sheets wouldn't fix him. I tried
anyway. They said
we were too young to fuck or die.
We fucked.
He died.
The house has no rules. Somewhere now
he sleeps with the dirt messing
his light hair like a grandfather's hand. And in his ex-home
his sister holds her shoulders on the couch, rocks
back and forth, humming. His mother stands
on the porch, screams
his name. 3:00 a.m. I hear
them, close the window,
hoping to close out
these new, selfish fears. I search
my breasts for hard spots like I
searched David's crotch with my mouth, looking
for one more year like a second date. Tonight I
touch myself, wish I
could kiss me.

The man who loves God
imagines my juices
and is frightened. He tells his minister
that my poems grow like wordy tumors. He tells
his mother that I need therapy. He searches
my lips for white stains. He searches
my weird skull
for horns.

The Orgasm I Didn't Have

The woman who lives below me is ninety-five.
Her face is hairier than her head.
She keeps her poodle, Ivan, close to her chest.
The two of them wear matching blue sweaters.

"Ivan was my husband's name," she said one afternoon.

Sometimes, late at night, I hear her.
"I, I, Ivan," she moans.

The men who lived in this apartment before me
used to fix things for her—her sink, vacuum,
and twin bed. Kindly, they gave her
their phone number, which has become
my phone number.

If I forget to take off my shoes or boots
and walk around the apartment, she calls immediately.

Last night, for the first time in months,
I brought a man home. It was midnight. I thought
we sang, undressed, and moved quietly.
I stifled myself for her.

She called in the morning, screamed her age
into my answering machine, and I blamed her
for the orgasm I didn't have.

Later, in the lobby, she shuffles by
in rubber boots, gossips to Ivan, pointing at me, and I think
of my friend Patricia, who, last month, was hit by a red truck,
thrown on top of the red truck like a tarp, bounced around
on her pretty blond head like a ping pong ball, finally
landing in the gutter with her ten acrylic nails
intact. She was twenty-nine.

I wanted that orgasm.
I needed it.
My whole day depended on it.

Did You Say Tramp?

I met him
in a bar. He's in bed
next to me. I smoke a fat joint
while he sleeps. I only suck
on the unworthy, prefer dragons
to gentlemen. Pull back the sheets,
take a look at his young ass. Tug
on his ear, judging him incompetent, write
my wrong number on a pad of paper
and go. Sex is always fine

the first time. I throw myself
into it, kiss his cement sides
and shaft—the chest I do not
like. I'm eating the butler
at midnight
with the hope
he'll clean my house.

Tony takes me flying
in his plane. He warns me
to give him head or die. I accept death
like a mattress
with blood stains. I cover this life
with a floral sheet. The plane dips
and bounces like an orgasm
or worse. This is really
about the dark, about no sparrow,
about not seeing flight
in anyone, about new blonds
with erections, promising things, about me
with all my distrust, accepting nothing. The wrong number
sits on the nightstand next to his skull. The wrong
number is the story of my bad life. I am not afraid
of abandonment. I'm afraid

of coffee in the morning. There's a cat here,
a bathrobe, white onions, and me. I'm six.
Run circles in the street. White car
hits me. I'm twenty-seven. This man
with his good body
on mine is a nightmare. He thinks
this scream
is an orgasm.
He's wrong.

If You Have Sex With Your Friend

—for Michael Tuitasi and Holly Haines

If you have sex with your friend
you know
it will change the color
of the air around him. The air
will go from plain air-color
to blue. And this blue
will outline your friend's face and neck and shoulders.
And the next time the two of you are being friendly, dining, in a room
full of other friends
he will mention, casually, a gifted woman from work
and you will see her
sitting in your baked potato
with her good legs crossed. You will look
at the blue around your friend's body
and grind your teeth. You will push
the plate away.

Even if you only mess around with your friend
you know
you will mess-up the friend part
and as hard as you try to return
to the time before the fondle
you will fail. You will look
at your friend at friend events
and your skin will twitch. And all you have
and have not done with your friend
will fill the front of your black bra.

If you have just kissed and touched your friend
you will fantasize
when he calls you on the phone.
Wrapping the cord around your finger
you will see his penis. He will ask you
for advice about women
and you will give it.

Later, you will sit
at a dinner party
and watch the woman's hand on your friend's leg.
You will hate the woman attached to the hand on your friend's leg.
You will hate the leg itself
for not wrapping around your own, for not
insisting on you.

Months after the fondle
you will go out with your friend to the friend bar.
You will sit with a bottle of beer in your hand
and suddenly you will remember the veins on his arms,
his Levis in a circle at his feet,
his wet face on your pillow.
And when the beer bottles are empty
and lined up, you will fixate
on your friend's lips. You will feel your tongue
inside your mouth. You will tell yourself
anything can survive
a night. You will tell yourself
air is never blue.

Censor

—for Steve Richmond

I wrote this poem called "If You Have Sex
With Your Friend," and it's a long poem,
one of my longest, and people seem
to like it, they say it's one of my
better poems, even my mother says, I like
that long poem, that poem about friendship.
And I say, Mom, that poem's about
sex. And she says, It is?

I was in New York when I wrote that poem.
I read it to my mom on the phone
and since she liked it
I sent her copies of the small press
which published the poem. When I
returned home this summer
for a visit, I found a copy
of it on the coffee table, right there,
next to *Time* and *Life,* and it meant
a lot to me, that she liked the poem
enough to display it. And then
last week, I picked the press up
from the coffee table, and looked
at my poem, read my poem
to myself, proud of myself
for writing that good, long poem
and when I got to the third stanza
I found that the word *penis*
had been blacked out
with such force
that the page opposite my poem
was stained. And I got up
from the couch, went to her room,
looked in her drawer, and found the other copies.
Yes, she'd used the black pen
again. And again. She'd done
what she's wanted to do
since my first period,
my first porch kiss.

Real Writer

My mother calls and tells me that my short story about the child left
on the freeway has come true, that in Los Angeles, a mother and
father did just that, left their three-year-old daughter on a freeway,
and my mother is almost happy telling the story, as if I knew
something deep and important by writing that story before the real
story happened, and how did I know that parents did things like that,
like deserting their little girl on a freeway, how did I know, how did I
predict the future, and maybe, she says, you're a witch, a psychic, or a
real writer after all.

4. MONSTERS AND OTHER LOVERS

Monsters and Other Lovers

Lorca and Sexton line
his bookshelves. On the left wall
his son's monster mask warns me. He stands
sideways, his shoulder against the sheer curtain
and says, "I want to climb out of this flesh
and into longevity; the men of my family
have clocks that go off
around forty." He touches his chest
where I want dinner
and sighs. At night
he holds his genitals
for fear they'll blow away
and turtles with their fine skins
whisper my name in his wife's ear.

Hungry

Monday night.
I'm at Safeway. I feel
the honeydew and a man comes up, winks
at me with green eyes and walks away. I pick up
ears of corn and another man comes up
and asks about my melons. I don't quite understand
this influx of attention, having been a shopper
for years and never been approached. Suddenly I realize
it's "date night" and these shoppers
are tired of barstools, numb soles,
and vodka. These shoppers
buy their food for the week
on the night
the hungry
come
out.

I leave with a guy
and a bottle of red wine. We go
to his apartment. The paint cracks
on all four walls. I comment
on his unfed plants. An insect
floats in a molded coffee cup and I'm happy here
in his mess
talking about toilet paper and garlic, unpacking his food
for the week. *People* magazine. He says he bought it
for the article on Bukowski. I tell him
he looks and walks like a writer. He shows me four poems.
Three are very good and I
kiss his cheek. We end up
rolling around on the bed. He tells me
he has only one ball.
I feel. Yes, one ball
but it's big. I show him
my scars and onions. He tells me
perfection is no great thing
and swallows my ear
like a vitamin.

When I Go Without Sex

When I go without sex
too long
my poems
like me
don't come
and it takes a certain
amount of nudity, death, onions,
or illness
to stir me into
a poem
and on Thursday night
a most unlikely man
did just that; he stirred me
out of the poet's bar and into
his living room and out of
my skirt and black boots and into
his sheets and sink and Levis and here it is
Sunday night
and he hasn't yet called.
By Monday I will hate him
and dry up
and if no one's dead or ill
the poems will stop
but today
I've written four.
Wow, what a guy.

Where My Spider Had Been

Lately I find myself loving
men who will not touch me: my cousin Steven,
a faithful professor who is not yet tenured,
an impotent physician in black Levis,
a crazy beauty who insists the vagina
is a big, hairy spider. My latest love
was a gypsy named Alix.

We drove across country, hooked
a wagon to my little car, left
California on a Thursday midnight.

"Women stink," he said
in Arizona. "I'm 30, a virgin,
and an atheist," he said
in New Mexico. In Texas
we became Alix Diddly
and Lisa Ray. In Oklahoma
we became a toothless couple
with tattooed genitals. In Boston
we became Cummings and Dickinson
and fucked
and fucked
and fucked
in a pink motel.

When we finished
he wanted to know
where my spider
had been. "How many
men?" he asked. And stupidly
I answered, "Fifteen." (Which was
itself
a kind lie.)

In New York
he ordered
twin beds.

Itch

She had an itch. It was in the middle of her back. A place she couldn't reach. She tried. She couldn't reach it. It was 12:00 a.m. A Friday. They were in bed, under the sheet, watching a talk show with the lights off. The man was laughing at the talk show, at the host. The host was talking about a fat woman in a red bikini on Malibu beach, how fat the woman was, how offended by her fat the host was, how every man on the beach was offended by the woman's fat.

Why? the man asked. Why would she wear that, you wouldn't wear a red bikini, not now, would you?

My back, she said, I have an itch, right here. And she had her arm twisted behind her, was pointing to the middle of her back where the itch was, saying, Right here, scratch it, ooh, please, right here.

I'm watching television, the man said. This guy's funny, I want to watch him.

Please, the woman said, scratch it, I'm itching.

And the man said, No. No, the man said.

Crank

On a Sunday in mid-November
the woman returns from church
and stands at her answering machine
listening. It is him
again. "My hard cock
and red, red balls insist
on you," he says.

He describes the black hairs
on his chest and ears.

He knows her name, says it twice
softly. "Virginia. Virginia."
Then, "Vagina."

The woman twists the purple beads
around her neck. She looks
around the room, searching
each corner for him.

In the bathroom she pulls
the shower curtain back
quickly, bravely, without
a weapon or a plan, just pulling
it back with her eyes large, with
her tongue hitting the back
of her bottom teeth, just pulling
the blue, plastic curtain back, as if
she might find him there
with his script, holding
her pink soap, as if
he might see her
and give up.

Substitute

Being a substitute teacher and a phone sex operator are miserable
jobs, both involve talking to people you wish were not talking, both
involve a calculated listening, both involve coaxing others into a
desired response, coming and learning equally necessary, you are
thinking, while the man on the phone

touches himself and wants you to be Jane as he swings from a palm
tree inside his BMW, as he sits in L.A. traffic on the 405 freeway,
loosening his tie, loosening his navy slacks, ambidextrous behind
his tinted windows and expensive shades, and you loosen too, in
your terry robe and apricot mask, wanting

to be anyone but who you are becoming, popping the chocolate in
your mouth at precisely the same time Tarzan pops out of his
briefs, and he is moaning and you are moaning, and outside your
bedroom window sits one red bird, a tiny boy on a bike—the candy

melting in your mouth is as creamy as Tarzan's hand will be, as his
belly, as his large wife at home once was, as the good soups she
now makes, and you are urging him on, for every minute is one
more dollar, one more piece of appreciation, adoration, and then
you break the rules, begging, saying

Don't hang up, don't leave me, please not yet, not now, anything
but that, please, and you hear yourself with the man you touch and
love reciting the same weak script,

it's all about disappearing and desertion, you are thinking, even
this chocolate spread out on your tongue now, the mask dry and
tight, curling at the edges of your aging face, the tiny boy riding
without hands, the man on the phone, his slow drive, the terrible
traffic, all the impatient people in cheaper cars right next to him,
on all four sides, surrounding him, the sweating blond to his left, so
close, so incredibly close he can almost

reach out his window and touch her cheek.

Threat

He threatens
to cut off
his balls. "All the men
are doing it," he says,
pointing to Hank's poem
in *Pearl* magazine. "If you need
the Reno Room, tequila, and new men
then the next time you come home
bring a pair of shears." I know

he is lying, of course,
because his balls
are his favorite things. He'd like
to have ten of them, each one
braver, bigger, more profound
than the next. He'd like

a grocery cart
to wheel around
his many balls. They'd fill
his Levis
like a sack
of red onions. They'd improve

his poetry, boost
his literary significance. His novel
would sit
on every shelf. Women

would come
by the dozens
to marvel. I'd be
the envy

of every Long Beach nightclub
and supermarket
for my man
with his stuffed briefs
would be loved.

MFA Program

The poetry students tell me
I have trouble
with my line breaks,
that my poems are easy,
uncomplicated, a simple woman's
reaction to her life.
They say, Your fiction is much better.

The fiction students tell me
my stories are too short
and lyrical, have no plot
or resolution, aren't stories
at all, but long poems.
They say, You're a much better poet.

New York City, In Freshly Painted Elevator With Old Woman and Dog

My ninety-five year old neighbor and I
move too slowly. She struggles with her dog
and bag of oranges. We stand
in the middle of the elevator,
so as not to smudge the paint.

Our shoulders are touching.

Even above the fumes
I smell her fruit
and mouth and poodle.

Somewhere around the third floor
the woman asks, Are you new here?

It is the same question
every time she sees me.

And though I've lived
in the building two years,
I always say, Yes.

A Woman Writing a Play

On a hot Saturday night in July the woman is home
typing. Her bedroom faces an alley. She hears
a cat fight, imagines claws and teeth, a pink collar,
some blood. And the couple across the way,
her least favorite neighbors, are screaming
again. "You're always drunk and ugly," Mrs. Billow says. "Because
you're always insignificant," Mr. Billow explains. And the woman

goes on typing, wiping her face now and then
with her palm, listening to the couple
who she knows will soon be fucking—all the time
thinking how silly
her play is, how little,
how indirect. But she

goes on typing and soon the couple
pants and climbs and soothes
and the cranky words they splattered
against their walls
turn to apologies. And the woman

goes on typing, trying to remember
the last time someone climbed her, soothed her
anywhere. She thinks that later she might
masturbate, setting his picture on the sheets, opening
a window, letting in the moon. And then

her little life, her play
begins. And she isn't sure *what*
is turning her on—the couple's moaning
had always disgusted her, the couple
had always turned her off. She'd seen them
on 2nd Street with their dressed-up poodle,

the woman's orange hair and big, selfish hat,
the man's tight mouth. And they never pleased her,
until now, until
this moment, until
their moans
became her own.

Walls

The walls
in my cheap apartment
are skinny. Every morning
and night I hear
the woman next door
enjoying her boyfriend's body.
She squeals and chirps
while I write horny poems.

Wednesday night I slept
on the porch, breathed vodka
onto a concrete pillow.

Tonight
the woman tells
her boyfriend, "The girl
next door who types
has weird eyes
and is a drunk."

I'd rather hear her
chirp and squeal.

Sweaty Roses

I hate flowers, really. If it's ever
my birthday and you want
to charm me, if you want me,
to take off my panties
buy me tequila.

When I lived in Hawaii
people gave leis. I was always bummed
when I got one. I'd get drunk
at the Wave and pull off
the petals. One new boy
who I never liked much
but slept with anyway
asked why I tortured roses.

"They stink," I said,
"and so do you—you don't wash
your balls often enough and
the women you admire
are stupid and useless."

He bought me another drink
and said, "You are
one of them."

Aspirin

I am always taking aspirin. My head
doesn't hurt, my back doesn't pound, no tooth
aches. I just
take aspirin. This habit
started after one night
of heavy tequila drinking.
I expected a headache. So, I took
four aspirin. Nothing happened; my head
didn't hurt; if my stomach bled
it didn't matter—I couldn't see it.
Nothing bruised or itched. He climbed
away from me, out my bedroom window
on a Friday night, bent my screen,
and left a hole
for insects, clouds, and other men.
Later, a spider crawled up my wall.
I smashed her with my brawling boot.
He called me a terrible drunk—his mad, dark fuck.
Her wet body in an X on my wall.
I took more aspirin.

Tonight, I'm in a bar
with my head chopped off
and in my lap. If I have a headache
I don't know it. I ask men
for aspirin
when I'm tired
of my life. I ask men
for aspirin
when I want
to be sucked on. I am always
taking aspirin.

He hands me the Sunday comics.
I am not laughing. I never laugh.
Tell me when it's funny
and I'll nod my head.

The blond boy eats me out,
perfectly, like a swimmer,
and I dry up. The dark one
touches my hand. I dig red nails
into his palm. When I like him
I hate him. When I'm naked
I'm mean. I invite the Reno Room
home to drink, serve ice water, and fall asleep
on my guests. At dawn I take four aspirin.
At noon I take two more.

I wait and wait
for my head to split.

Her Spot

I like my blue sheets
because they remind me
of water, I tell him, in the middle
of things. He's on me now
for the second time.
It is morning.
The sun beats on us as we
beat on and in each other.
The walls are dirty.
A hickey sits on his neck.
It comes from someone else.
I circle her hickey
with my tongue; I suck on her
hickey, her spot, her mark.
The walls are dirty.
I see footprints.
I see eggshells.
I must clean the walls
when he is through.

Cutting Yourself

It's like looking at the sun without sunglasses, though you know it's unhealthy, though it's painful, looking right at the sun for as long as you can, proving something, it's like eating a box of cookies, though four are plenty and your dress will never fit on Friday, it's like that, it's like fucking Kevin's best friend when it's Kevin you want, it's like never telling Kevin you want him and becoming a bully when he doesn't guess, like complaining about bald men in general when Kevin's losing his curls, it's like kneeling on the black and white tile, your middle finger at the back of your throat, watching the cookies fly, thinking about all your Kevins, it's like bringing a stranger home from the supermarket because of his Levis, like refusing to look at his penis or balls for fear you might miss them later, like drinking so much tequila and beer if he kills you it won't hurt, like telling him to keep his name and musical taste to himself, it's like that, it's like waiting all year for your birthday, and when it finally comes, insisting on staying home, it's like that night, turning twenty-five in the garage, sitting on top of the dryer with a bobby pin between your fingers, biting off the soft part, spitting it out, letting the phone ring and ring, because all you want to do is this, just this.

Lisa Glatt was born in 1963 and has spent most of her life
in Southern California. She has an MFA from Sarah Lawrence
College and currently teaches writing at California State
University, Long Beach, and in the UCLA Extension Writers'
Program.